D0364758

AS SEEN ON DVD!
KING OF THE RAILWAY
THE MOVIE

TREASURE ON THE TRACKS

Based on The Railway Series
by The Reverend W Awdry

Illustrated by Richard Courtney

Random House 🏠 New York

Bring the soap!

Bring the water!

Scrub, rinse, and repeat.

Dear Parent:

Congratulations! Your child is taking the first steps on an exciting journey. The destination? Independent reading!

STEP INTO READING® will help your child get there. The program offers five steps to reading success. Each step includes fun stories and colorful art. There are also Step into Reading Sticker Books, Step into Reading Math Readers, Step into Reading Phonics Readers, Step into Reading Write-In Readers, and Step into Reading Phonics Boxed Sets—a complete literacy program with something for every child.

Learning to Read, Step by Step!

Ready to Read Preschool–Kindergarten
• big type and easy words • rhyme and rhythm • picture clues
For children who know the alphabet and are eager to begin reading.

Reading with Help Preschool–Grade 1
• basic vocabulary • short sentences • simple stories
For children who recognize familiar words and sound out new words with help.

Reading on Your Own Grades 1–3
• engaging characters • easy-to-follow plots • popular topics
For children who are ready to read on their own.

Reading Paragraphs Grades 2–3
• challenging vocabulary • short paragraphs • exciting stories
For newly independent readers who read simple sentences with confidence.

Ready for Chapters Grades 2–4
• chapters • longer paragraphs • full-color art
For children who want to take the plunge into chapter books but still like colorful pictures.

STEP INTO READING® is designed to give every child a successful reading experience. The grade levels are only guides. Children can progress through the steps at their own speed, developing confidence in their reading, no matter what their grade.

Remember, a lifetime love of reading starts with a single step!

Thomas the Tank Engine & Friends™

CREATED BY BRITT ALLCROFT

Based on The Railway Series by the Reverend W Awdry.
© 2013 Gullane (Thomas) LLC.
Thomas the Tank Engine & Friends and Thomas & Friends are trademarks of
Gullane (Thomas) Limited.
HIT and the HIT Entertainment logo are trademarks of HIT Entertainment Limited.
All rights reserved. Published in the United States by Random House Children's Books,
a division of Random House, Inc., 1745 Broadway, New York, 10019, and in Canada by
Random House of Canada Limited, Toronto.

Step into Reading, Random House, and the Random House colophon are registered trademarks of
Random House, Inc.

Visit us on the Web!
StepIntoReading.com
randomhouse.com/kids
www.thomasandfriends.com

Educators and librarians, for a variety of teaching tools, visit us at
RHTeachersLibrarians.com

ISBN 978-0-449-81535-9 (trade) — ISBN 978-0-375-97168-6 (lib. bdg.)
Printed in the United States of America
10 9 8 7 6 5 4 3 2 1

HiT entertainment

The engines are
squeaky-clean.
They are
ready to greet
a special guest.

The guest is
the Earl of Sodor.

The earl
tells the engines
about his special plan.

He will rebuild
the old castle.
Thomas will help.

Thomas and Percy
chuff up the hill.
The castle is old.

The walls are broken.
There is rubble
all around.

Thomas takes
a closer look.

It is not rubble.

It is treasure!

He finds armor.

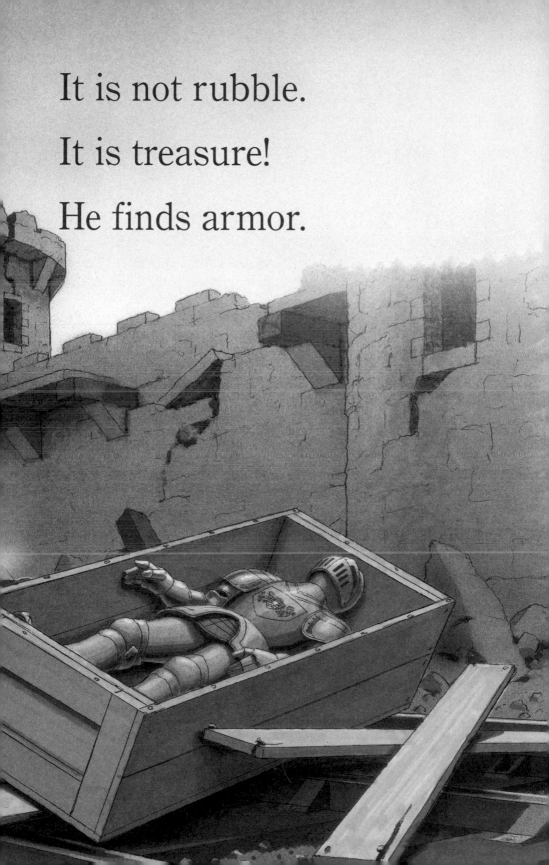

The earl has
a special engine.
His name is Stephen.

Stephen is old.

He needs repairs, too.

Thomas brings Stephen to the Steamworks.

Clink! Clang! Clunk!
Victor makes Stephen
as good as new.

Stephen wants to help.
What job can he do?

Some engines
make repairs.
Stephen cannot reach.

Some engines
carry cargo.
Stephen cannot
carry much.

Some engines
move stone.
The stone is too heavy
for Stephen.

Stephen is sad.

He chuffs off alone.

Uh-oh!

Trucks are coming.

Look out, Stephen!

CRASH!

Thomas searches

for Stephen.

Stephen is safe!
And he found
something special.

It is a king's crown!
It belongs
at the castle.

The earl gives Stephen his new job.

He has the perfect job.

He helps at the castle!

Hooray for Stephen!